THE YOUNG INDIANA JONES CHRONICLES

Safari in Africa

In 1909, when this story takes place, people felt that the best way to preserve wildlife was to kill wild animals and display them in museums. In this way people visiting the museums could see and understand these animals. President Theodore Roosevelt believed this idea strongly. In fact, he was given many awards from environmental groups for his work in "collecting" animals for museums. Today we believe that wildlife should be protected, and we have laws that prohibit hunters from shooting and selling wild animals.

THE YOUNG INDIANA JONES CHRONICLES

Safari in Africa

Adapted by Sally Bell

Illustrated by Gonzalez Vincente

A Lucasfilm Ltd. Production
THE YOUNG INDIANA JONES CHRONICLES™
Starring Sean Patrick Flanery, Corey Carrier, Margaret Tyzack, Ronny
Coutteure, Ruth De Sosa, Lloyd Owen, and George Hall as "Old Indy"
Director of Photography David Tattersall, Oliver Stapleton, Miguel Icaza
Solana, Jorgen Persson, and Giles Nuttgens
Edited by Edgar Burcksen, Louise Rubacky, and Ben Burtt
Production Designer Gavin Bocquet
Costume Designer Charlotte Holdich
Music by Laurence Rosenthal and Joel McNeely
Executive Producer George Lucas
Produced by Rick McCallum
Written by Jonathan Hales, Rosemary Anne Sisson, Reg Gadney,
Jonathan Hensleigh, Matthew Jacobs, Carrie Fisher, Frank Darabont,
and Gavin Scott
Based on a Story by George Lucas
Directed by Jim O'Brien, Carl Schultz, Rene Manzor, Bille August,
Nicolas Roeg, Simon Wincer, Terry Jones, Gavin Millar, Vic Armstrong,
and Deepa Mehta
Copyright Lucasfilm Ltd.
Produced in Association with Amblin Television and Paramount
Television

A GOLDEN BOOK • NEW YORK
Western Publishing Company, Inc., Racine, Wisconsin 53404

British East Africa
1909

"This is incredible!" said nine-year-old Indiana Jones as he looked out over the African wilderness. He was traveling through Africa with his parents and his tutor, Miss Seymour. Indy thought Africa was beautiful— and there were so many animals! Best of all, he was going on a safari with former President Teddy Roosevelt himself!

The boy got down from his horse and began to unpack in a hurry.

"Slow down, Henry," said Miss Seymour. She always called him by his real name. "This wilderness has been here for millions of years. It's not going to disappear while you unpack."

"No, but I may miss seeing Mr. Roosevelt return from the hunt," answered Indy. He quickly finished unpacking and set off to explore the camp.

Indy discovered a large, open tent. His
father and another man were inside.

"Henry, this is Dr. Heller," said Professor
Jones. "After the hunters shoot the animals,
he prepares them for the museums."

Dr. Heller smiled at Indy. "Next time you
go into a museum and stare at a lion, you can
think of me," he said.

"I will," Indy said with a laugh.

Then Indy went outside again. He climbed to the top of a nearby hill and looked around. Down below, he saw a village.

Indy started down the hill toward the village. Then he stopped. Someone was watching him. It was a boy—a Masai boy who was just about his age.

Eagerly, Indy headed toward the boy. But
then he heard Miss Seymour calling him. The
hunting party had returned! Indy ran back to
the camp.

After dinner that evening, Mr. Roosevelt
showed Indy a book that had a picture of an
animal called a Burton's oryx. It looked like
a deer with very unusual fringed ears.
"Thousands of these animals live in Africa,"
he said. "But we haven't seen any yet."

"It's beautiful," whispered Indy.

The next day Mr. Roosevelt taught Indy
how to shoot a gun. Then he gave Indy a
pair of binoculars. "You will not be coming
on today's hunt with us," said Mr. Roosevelt,
"but you should at least be able to see this
fine land."

Indy wanted to look for the Burton's oryxes. He took a notebook, which had a picture of the animal in it, and the binoculars, and ran to the hill he had climbed the day before. He hoped he would see the Masai boy again. And there he was—watching for Indy.

Indy pointed to himself. "Indy," he said.

"Indy?" the boy repeated. Indy nodded and smiled.

Just then some men called, "Meto!" The boy waved to them.

"Meto?" said Indy. "Is that your name?" The boy smiled. Indy showed him the binoculars. Meto had never seen anything like them before.

Meto said something in an excited voice and pulled at Indy's arm. Together the two boys ran across the plains and climbed another hill.

In the valley below was a water hole with all kinds of animals around it. "Gosh!" whispered Indy as he looked at them through his binoculars.

Suddenly Indy spotted a lion! Through the
binoculars it looked as if it were right on top
of the boys. Indy started to jump up, but Meto
used hand signs to tell him to stay still.

Indy could hardly believe his eyes! The lion
walked right past them and didn't even look
their way! They watched the lion stalk and
kill an antelope. Indy decided he would try to
learn Meto's language so that Meto could tell
him important things like "Don't move!"

Later that day Mr. Roosevelt brought the heads of two white rhinos into camp. "This animal is very rare," he said proudly. "There are only a few left. We've killed seven of them."

"But why?" asked Indy. "Why do you want to kill such a rare animal?"

"Because people need to see and understand the wilderness, Henry," said Mr. Roosevelt. "If they see examples of rare animals in a museum, maybe they will try to save the ones that are left."

That evening Mr. Roosevelt asked Indy to
play a game of checkers. "My move, Henry?"
asked Mr. Roosevelt.

"Yes, sir," Indy replied. He watched Mr.
Roosevelt make his move. "I've been thinking
about the Burton's oryxes, sir," Indy said. "I
think I could find them for you."

Mr. Roosevelt smiled. "You could, eh?
Well, we need one for the museum. I'll count
on you."

"Then I promise I'll find them," Indy said.
He watched as Mr. Roosevelt jumped all the
rest of his pieces.

"This is a Burton's oryx," Indy told Meto
the next day. He showed Meto the picture of
the animal. He tried to say it in Meto's
language, but he didn't know enough words.

"Oryx," said Meto in his own language.
He studied the picture. Then he pointed to
a cliff and gestured for Indy to follow him.
Meto began to climb. Indy started up the
cliff after him.

Suddenly a big snake slithered up to Indy. Slowly it coiled itself around him. "Meto, help!" yelled Indy.

Meto quickly grabbed a stick and hit the snake. The snake let go of Indy and fell into the valley below. Meto once again led the way and Indy followed him.

When Indy at last reached the top of the cliff, he couldn't see Meto anywhere. "Meto!" he shouted.

Meto poked his head out of a nearby cave and grinned. He led Indy into the cave and proudly showed him a picture of some Burton's oryxes painted on the wall.

Indy was disappointed. "But where is a *live* one?" he asked.

Meto took Indy to the Masai village. There they showed Indy's picture of the Burton's oryx to a wise woman. The old woman nodded and led them out onto the plains again. Many of the villagers followed.

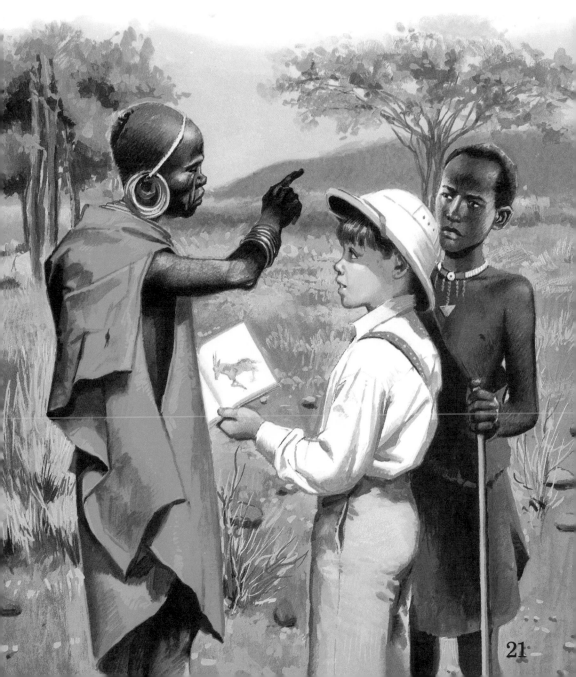

Back at the camp, Miss Seymour was looking all over for Indy. It was time for his lessons, but she couldn't find him anywhere.

Miss Seymour ran to Professor and Mrs. Jones. Mr. Roosevelt was with them. "I can't find Henry!" she said. "I haven't seen him for hours."

"We can't have that," said Mr. Roosevelt. "We'll have to send out a search party. I certainly hope he hasn't gone far."

Mr. Roosevelt rode off into the wilderness, followed by the search party.

Meanwhile Indy, Meto, and the Masai villagers had arrived at a big tree. There was an old, old man sitting under it, playing a flute. "Laibon!" said the old woman.

Indy sat down in front of the Laibon, the wise man. He showed the Laibon his picture of the Burton's oryx.

The Laibon studied the picture. "Oryx," he said in his own language.

Indy watched as the Laibon drew in the sand. The drawings showed Indy what had happened to the oryxes. Slowly, with Meto's help, Indy began to understand.

The Laibon was pleased that Indy
understood. He made some more drawings.
Indy and the Laibon were so absorbed that
they did not notice when Meto left them.

Suddenly Indy saw that it was dark. Meto
was nowhere to be seen.

"Gosh, it's late. I have to get back!" he said.
"Thank you!" Indy ran toward the camp alone.

It was dark on the plains. Indy couldn't see anything. He heard strange noises all around him. All of a sudden someone grabbed him! Indy screamed. Then he saw that it was one of the searchers from the camp! The man smiled at him.

The searcher brought Indy back to the camp. Mrs. Jones rushed to meet them. She hugged Indy. Then she shook him. "How could you, Henry!" she cried. "We've been so worried."

Mr. Roosevelt was there, too. "I'm disappointed in you, Henry," said Mr. Roosevelt. "I thought you were smarter."

"But, sir, I was trying to find the Burton's oryx for you," cried Indy.

But Mr. Roosevelt didn't seem to care. He looked at Professor Jones. "You'd better keep a closer eye on your son after this. The African wilderness is not a playground."

"You can be sure I will," said Professor Jones. He took Indy to his tent. "You're going to bed without any supper, my boy."

In his tent Indy sat on his bed and studied his picture of the oryx. "Why won't they even listen?" he wondered.

Then he turned out his flashlight. He drifted off to sleep, thinking about the oryx, hearing the unfamiliar noises of Africa all around him.

Suddenly Indy heard a different noise.
Something was moving right next to his tent!
Indy lay very still, hoping it would go away.
Instead, it stopped outside his tent flap. The
flap opened. Indy scrambled under the bed.

Meto walked into the tent. "Come," he
said in his own language. "We have to find
the oryx!"

"Well . . ." said Indy. He looked outside.
No one else was awake. "All right, I'll go!"

Indy and Meto ran across the plains to the forest. High up in the trees, Indy could hear monkeys chattering, but he couldn't see them. It was barely light.

At last the boys came out of the forest. They were on top of a huge cliff. The sun was just rising. "Gosh!" said Indy. "It's magnificent."

"Come on, Indy!" said Meto in his own language. He led the way to a small green valley in the cliffside. He had found the melons that oryxes like to eat!

The boys settled down behind some bushes. Indy scanned the horizon through his binoculars.

Soon Meto saw a movement. He touched Indy's arm and pointed. Indy raised his binoculars.

A Burton's oryx peeked out from the bushes. Then it delicately stepped into the valley. Three more oryxes followed. They dug in the ground for a melon and began to eat it.

The boys watched for a time. Then they quietly got up and headed back to camp. They had a plan.

Indy crept back into his tent without being seen. Then he came out of the tent, yawning, as if he had just woken up.

Mr. Roosevelt saw him. "I hope you've learned your lesson, Henry," said Mr. Roosevelt.

"Yes, sir, I did," said Indy.

Suddenly Meto rushed up. He was holding a melon. "Indy! Indy!" Meto cried.

"Wait, Meto, I'm telling him," said Indy in Meto's language. He took the melon from Meto and gave it to Mr. Roosevelt. Then he gestured to Meto and said, "Sir, this is my friend Meto. He's been helping me."

"Helping you with what?" asked Mr. Roosevelt.

Indy explained. "I found out that Burton's oryxes eat these melons."

"They do?" asked Professor Jones.

"Yes, Dad," Indy said. Then he told them what he had learned from the Laibon's drawings. "A long time ago there was a fire that killed a lot of snakes," Indy explained. "The snakes used to eat mole rats, so there got to be too many mole rats. Mole rats feed on these melons, too, and they ate most of them. So the oryxes died out."

"All of them?" asked Professor Jones.

"No, some of the oryxes survived, and Meto helped me find them."

"Hmmm," said Mr. Roosevelt. "Can you show us where they are?"

"Yes, sir, we can!" Indy said proudly.

"You have a very bright lad here, Professor Jones," said Mr. Roosevelt.

That morning a hunting party set out. Indy and Meto rode ahead of everyone. Mr. Roosevelt and his son, Kermit, rode just behind them.

"Are you sure this is the place, Henry?" Mr. Roosevelt asked quietly when they reached the green valley.

"Yes, sir, this is it," replied Indy.

They left the horses at the top of the valley walls. The hunters took their guns and waited behind the bushes.

Indy looked at all the guns. "Is everyone going to shoot?" he asked.

"Shhh!" said Mr. Roosevelt.

Everyone was quiet.

Meto and Indy watched as three oryxes emerged slowly from the bushes. More oryxes followed them.

Suddenly there was a blast as Mr. Roosevelt fired. An oryx fell dead. Quickly more shots rang out and two more oryxes fell.

Indy saw Mr. Roosevelt aiming at another oryx. "Stop!" Indy shouted. "You've killed too many already. Don't shoot any more!"

The shooting stopped. In the silence that followed, the remaining oryxes ran to safety.

Mr. Roosevelt looked furious. But before he could say anything, Indy continued, "Sir, if you kill any more, there might be none left."

Mr. Roosevelt was thoughtful. "You're right, Henry," he said after a while. "Other animals might depend on these oryxes being here."

Indy watched the hunters lift the dead oryxes and tie them onto the horses. He felt sad. "They were so beautiful," he said softly.

Mr. Roosevelt came up behind Indy and put his hand on his shoulder. "Thank you, my boy," he said.

"Yes, sir," said Indy. Then he looked up at the top of the hill. He could see the rest of the oryxes moving quickly away. Meto saw them, too. He and Indy looked at each other but said nothing.

A few days later Indy and the rest of the hunting party packed up their camp. Indy went to find Meto.

"I came to say good-bye," said Indy in Masai. "We're leaving today."

Indy took the binoculars and put them around Meto's neck. Meto looked through them. Then he gave Indy his flute. It was just like the one the Laibon had played. Indy played a little tune on it.

Miss Seymour called, "Henry! We're ready to go!" Indy hesitated. Then he rushed back up the hill to join the rest of the group.

As he rode away from the empty camp, Indy could see Meto watching. Indy waved to him.

Through his binoculars, Meto watched Indy's group move away until they were only specks on the vast African plains.